# THE DINOSAUR THAT POOPED A REINDEER!

## Tom Fletcher and Dougie Poynter
### Illustrated by Garry Parsons

PUFFIN

One Christmas, a note from the North Pole arrived
for Danny and Dino - but what was inside?

To Mr
To Danny & Dino
NORTH POLE POST

They boarded the North Pole Express in the snow.
Dino was hungry, but Danny cried, "NO!"

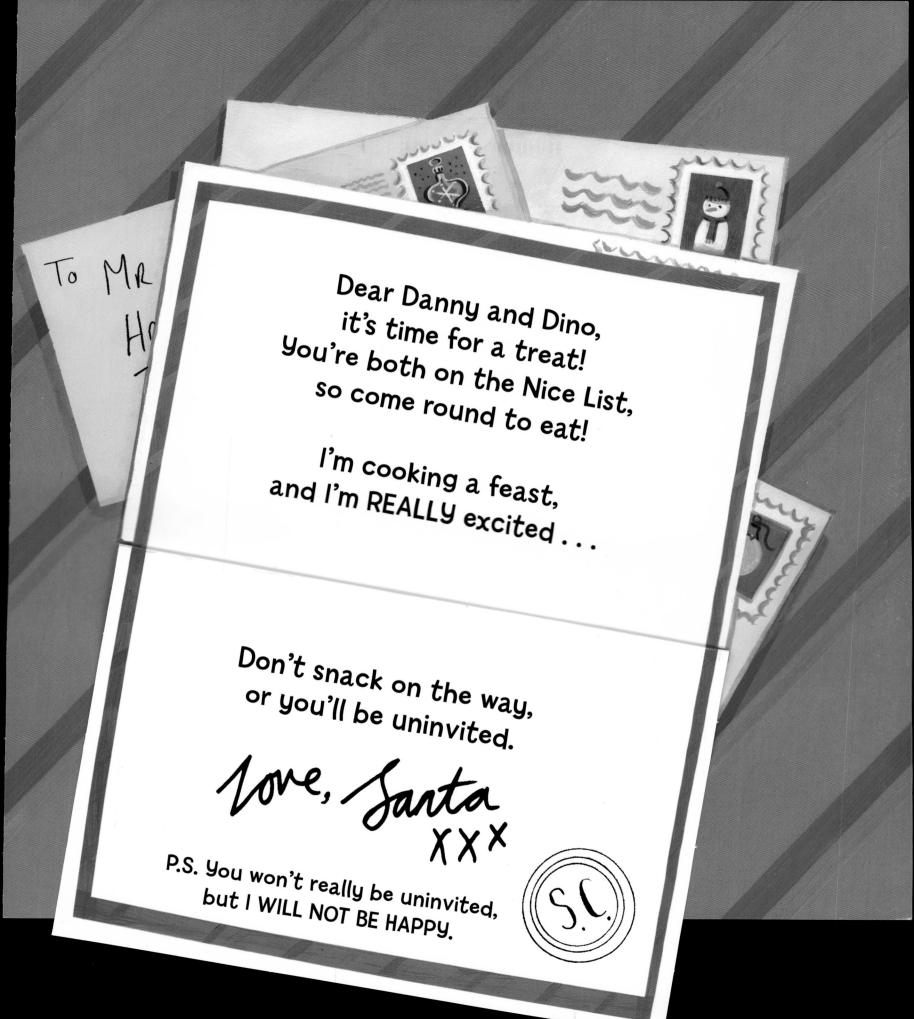

They boarded the North Pole Express in the snow.
Dino was hungry, but Danny cried, **"NO!"**

The train rushed through forests with candy-cane trees,

then mountains of crackers with houses of cheese.

With rumbling tummies, the pair remained strong
and didn't snack once as the train chugged along.

With one final *CHUFF*, the express train pulled in.
"You're here!" Santa cried, with a big jolly grin.

KITCHEN

WORKSH

"The feast's almost ready,
but there's time before . . .

# HARE
### AND
# TORTOISE

For Beth

ORCHARD BOOKS
338 Euston Road, London NW1 3BH
*Orchard Books Australia*
17/207 Kent Street, Sydney, NSW 2000

First published in 2015 by Orchard Books

ISBN 978 1 40831 308 4

Text and illustrations © Alison Murray 2015

The right of Alison Murray to be identified as the
author and illustrator of this book has been asserted
by her in accordance with the Copyright, Designs
and Patents Act, 1988.

A CIP catalogue record for this book is available from the British Library.

1 3 5 7 9 10 8 6 4 2

Printed in China

Orchard Books is a division of Hachette Children's Books,
an Hachette UK company.

www.hachette.co.uk

# Hare
## AND
# Tortoise

Retold by
Alison Murray

ORCHARD

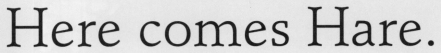

# Here comes Hare.

Hello, Hare.

# Hey, Hare. Hellooo!

Could you stand still for a
minute please, Hare?

# The Hare

### genus leapus swifticus

**Ears**

Accustomed to the sound of animals cheering

**Eyes**

Sharply focused on the finish line

**Head**

Perhaps a little bit big

**Nose**

Ready to sniff out another victory

**Whiskers**

Extra twitchy

**Paws**

Used to crossing finish line in first place

**Hind Legs**

Coiled like springs, ready to leap into action

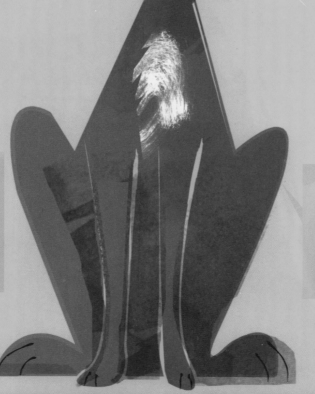

# Meet Hare.

Hare can barely stay still for a minute, but he can:

* Run through the tickliest grass

* Rush around rivers and ponds

* Nip over misty meadows

(And he has NEVER been known to resist a carrot.)

"I'm the fastest on the farm.

No one can beat me!" says Hare.

Today, Hare will be racing . . .

. . . Tortoise.

Has anyone seen Tortoise?

Tortoise, where are you?

Ah! There she is!

# The Tortoise
## genus slow and steadicus

fig 1. Tortoise

fig 2. Rock

# Meet Tortoise.

Tortoise *can* stay still for a VERY long time

but she has never been known to:

❋ Run through the tickliest grass

❋ Rush around rivers and ponds

❋ Nip over misty meadows

(But she will always do her best.)


"I may be slow but I'll give it a go," smiles Tortoise.


Let the race begin!

"Let's race to the gate," smiles Hare, with a twitch of his whiskers. "First one there wins, so that will be me!"

"We'll see," nods Tortoise.

When the cock crows, the race is on.

Ready . . .

Steady . . .

The Race Course

The Duck Pond

Start

Finish

The Carrot Field

The Shady Tree

The Meadow

Cock-a-

Oh!

doodle-GO!

Byeee!

Hare races through the tickliest grass.

Tortoise trundles through the tickliest grass.

"I'm so fast, I fly past," sings Hare.

"I may be slow, but watch me go," hums Tortoise.

Hare is out of the meadow and zipping past the duck pond.

Oh dear, Tortoise is *not* out of the meadow . . .

"I'm so fast, I fly past," sings Hare.

"I may be slow, but watch me go," hums Tortoise.

Hare reaches the carrot field.
(Remember, Hare can never resist a carrot.)
"I'm so fast . . . huh? CARROTS!" gasps Hare.
"Tortoise is *miles* behind, so I'll have time
for a few nibbles . . .

. . . and a tiny nap under
the shady tree."

But where is Tortoise?

Ah, at last she trundles
out of the meadow . . .

. . . she tootles
around the duck pond . . .

. . . she tiptoes through the carrot field . . .
(Just look at her go!)

. . . and right past Hare, who sleeps on, dreaming of winning races and animals cheering.

"Hang on
a minute!"
gasps Hare.
"Animals cheering?"

Hare hurries!

Hare races!

Hare chases!

But Tortoise has won by a whisker!

"Hare, you may be fast,"
smiles Tortoise.
"But I walked straight past!"

Poor Hare. He's not used to losing.

"Never mind, Hare, you might
just win next time," says Tortoise.
"Come on . . .

. . . race you to the lettuce patch!"

# The Race Course

The Carrot Field

The Duck Pond

The Meadow

Start